BERNARD'S NAP

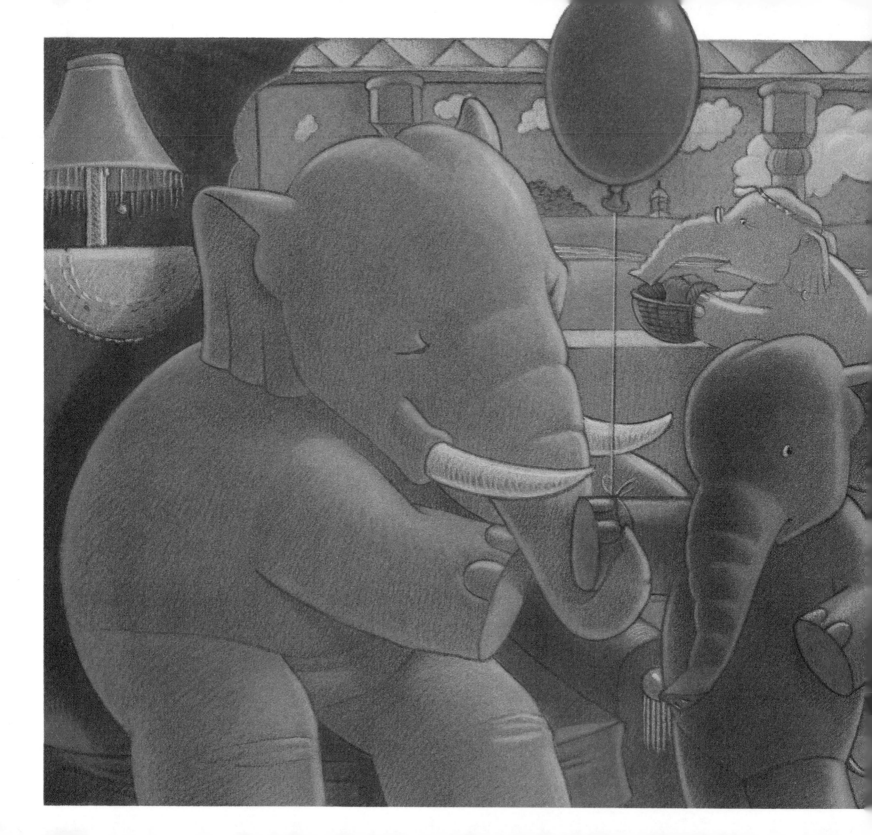

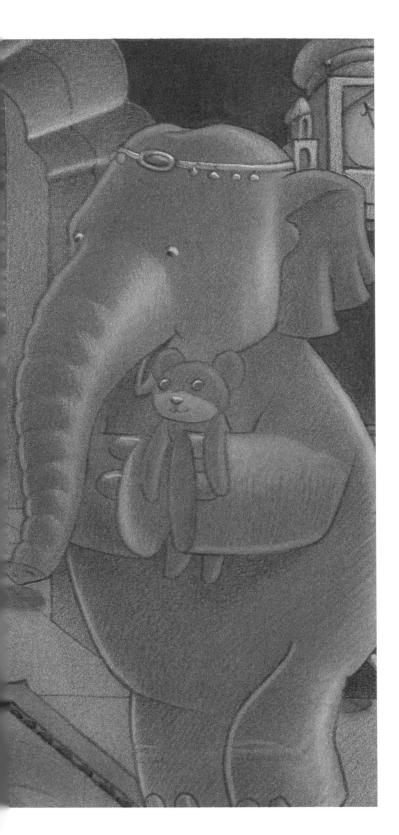

BERNARD'S NAP

BY JOAN ELIZABETH GOODMAN

ILLUSTRATED BY
DOMINIC CATALANO

BOYDS MILLS PRESS

For Becky
         —J. E. G.

In loving memory of my grandmother
              —D. C.

Text copyright © 1999 by Joan Elizabeth Goodman
Illustrations copyright © 1999 by Dominic Catalano

This book is a presentation of Atlas Editions, Inc.
For more information about Atlas Editions
book clubs for children write to: Atlas Editions, Inc.,
4343 Equity Drive, Columbus, Ohio 43228.
2000 Edition
Printed in the USA

Publisher Cataloging-in-Publication Data

Goodman, Joan Elizabeth
   Bernard's nap / by Joan Elizabeth Goodman ; illustrated by
Dominic Catalano.—1st ed.
[32]p. : col. Ill. ; cm.
Summary: A young elephant refuses to take his nap, despite the efforts
of his parents and grandmother.
ISBN 1-56397-728-1
1. Elephants—Fiction—Juvenile literature. 2. Bedtime—Fiction—
Juvenile literature [1. Elephants—Fiction. 2. Bedtime—Fiction.]
I. Catalano, Dominic, ill. II. Title
   [E]-dc21 1999 AC CIP
Library of Congress Catalog Card Number 98-071790

First edition, 1999
Book designed by Dominic Catalano and Tim Gillner
The text of this book is set in 20-point Galliard.
The illustrations are done in pastels.

10 9 8 7 6 5 4 3 2 1

"Nap time!" said Mama.
"Not sleepy," said Bernard.
"Of course you are," said Papa. "It's nap time!"

Mama put Bernard in his bed. She tucked Mr. Bear in beside him, and gave Bernard two sleep kisses.

Grandma covered Bernard with his blanket.

"Happy nap, Bernard," said Mama.

"No nap," said Bernard, and he stood up. "Play blocks."

"Lie down and go to sleep," said Papa.

"NOT SLEEPY!" said Bernard.

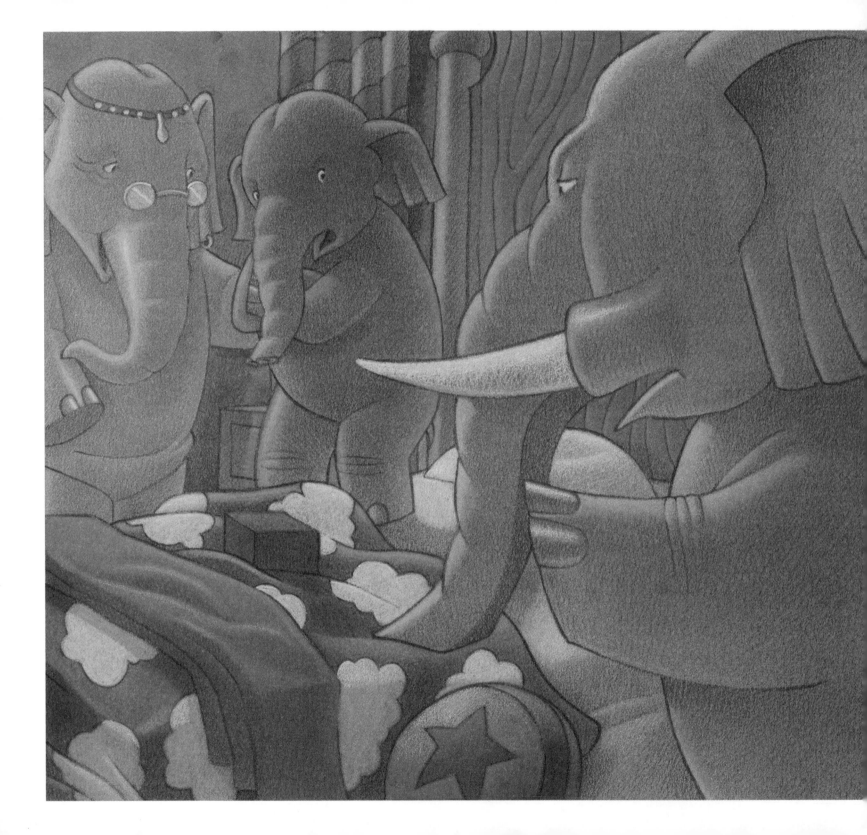

"No need to shout," said Grandma.

"I will sing you the 'Elephant's Lullaby,' " said Mama. "That will help you go to sleep."

Bernard sat down. Mama sang:

"Down by the river
where the breeze is cool,
the elephants gather
near the biggest pool.

They rock-a-bye their babies
in softly swinging beds,
crooning 'La, la, lo, lo,
sleep, little sleepyheads.

La, la, lo, lo,
la, la, lo.
Sleep, sweetly sleep
rocking to and fro.
La, la, la, la,
la, la, lo.' "

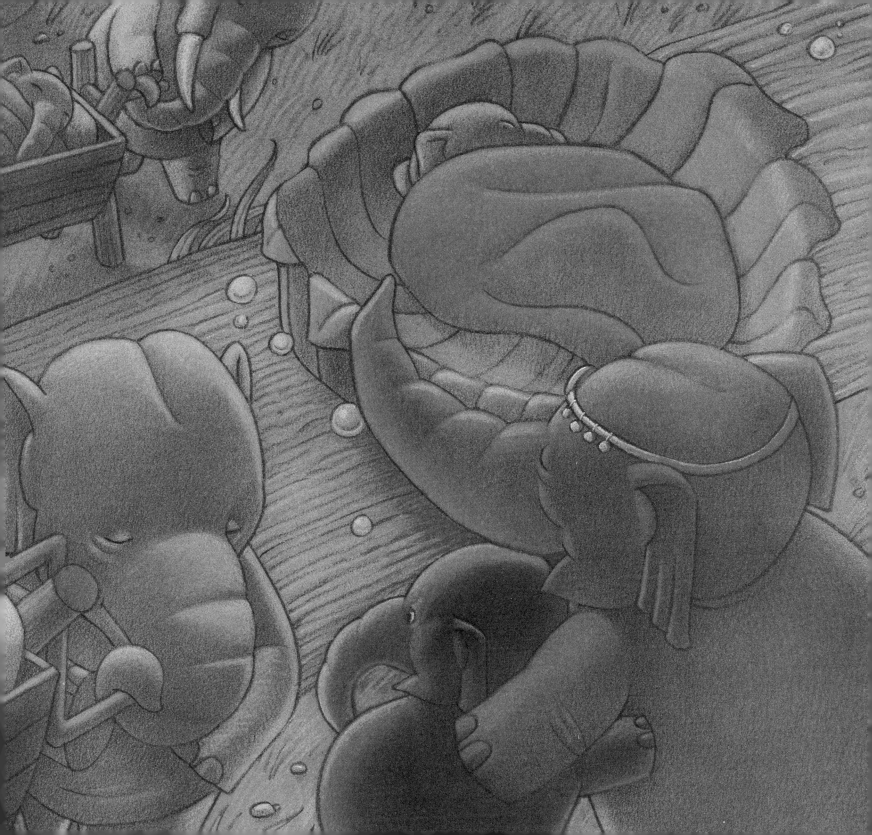

Mama yawned a great yawn and rubbed her eyes.

"Now you can go to sleep," she said.

"No," said Bernard.

"Then Papa will tell you a sleepy story while I have a little lie-down," said Mama.

"Not sleepy," said Bernard.

"You will be," said Papa, and he told Bernard this story:

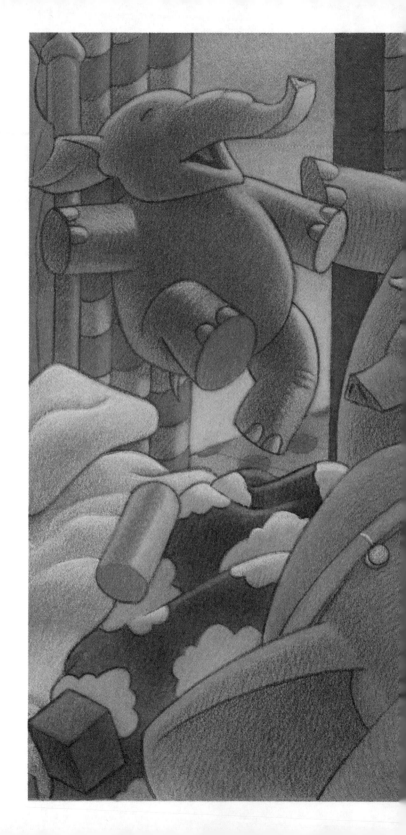

"Once there was a tiny little house
    with two tiny windows
    and a tiny little door.
    Inside the tiny little house
    there lived a sleepy, sleepy mouse
    who had a tiny little bed
    and a soft, soft pillow
    for his tired, tired head."

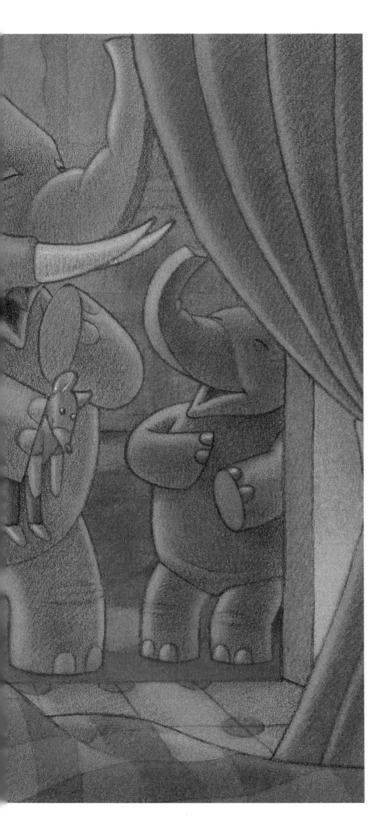

"Are you getting sleepy?" asked Papa.

"No!" said Bernard.

"Well, the mouse is very sleepy," Papa yawned. "And so am I."

"Not I," said Bernard.

"I will sit in the rocking chair by Bernard's bed and knit," said Grandma. "That will soothe Bernard and help him go to sleep."

"Then I will have a little snooze," said Papa. Grandma sat in the rocking chair.

Click, click, click went Grandma's knitting needles. *Crick, creek* went the rocking chair. "Knit one, purl one," said Grandma. *Click, click, click. Crick, creek.* "Knit one, purl one." *Crick, creek. Crick, creek.*

Grandma's head began to nod. And soon she was fast asleep.

Bernard got out of bed and took Mr. Bear to find Mama. She was snoring softly in her bed. Bernard tucked Mr. Bear in beside Mama and gave her two sleep kisses.

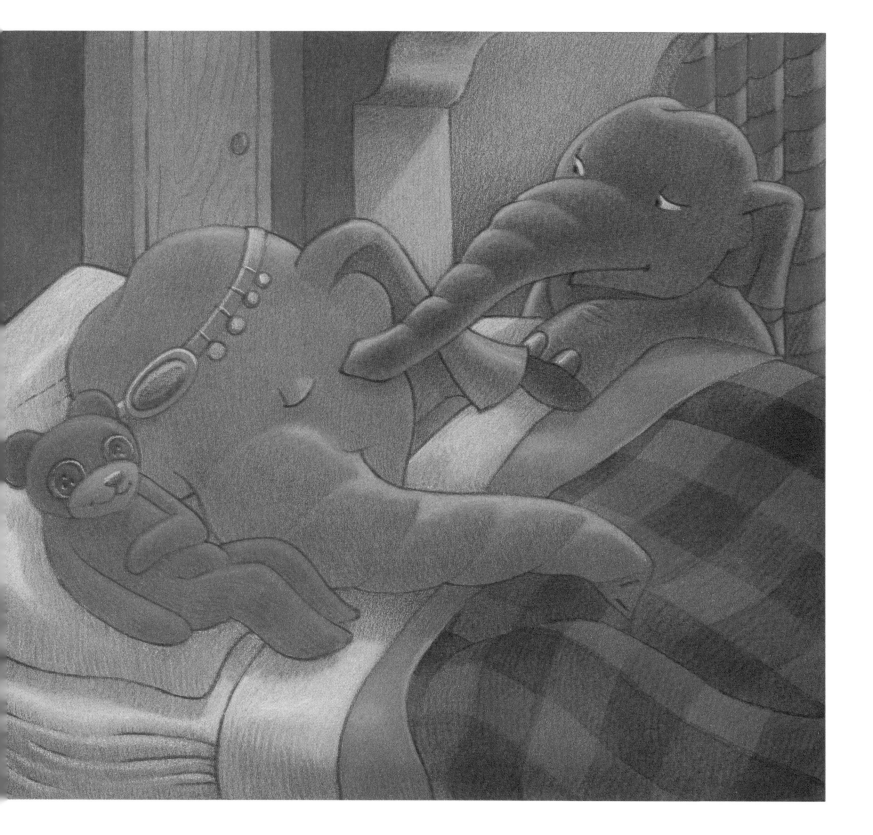

Bernard found Papa in the den. He was snoring loudly in his chair. Bernard got out his blocks. He made a house for Papa. He made the walls tall. He made two big windows for Papa, and a wide door. When he was done, Bernard went back to his room.

Grandma was still asleep in the rocking chair. Bernard put his blanket across her lap.

Then Bernard climbed into bed. He watched the cranes on his mobile fly round and round. He sang himself a little song:

"La, la, lo, lo,
la, la, lo."

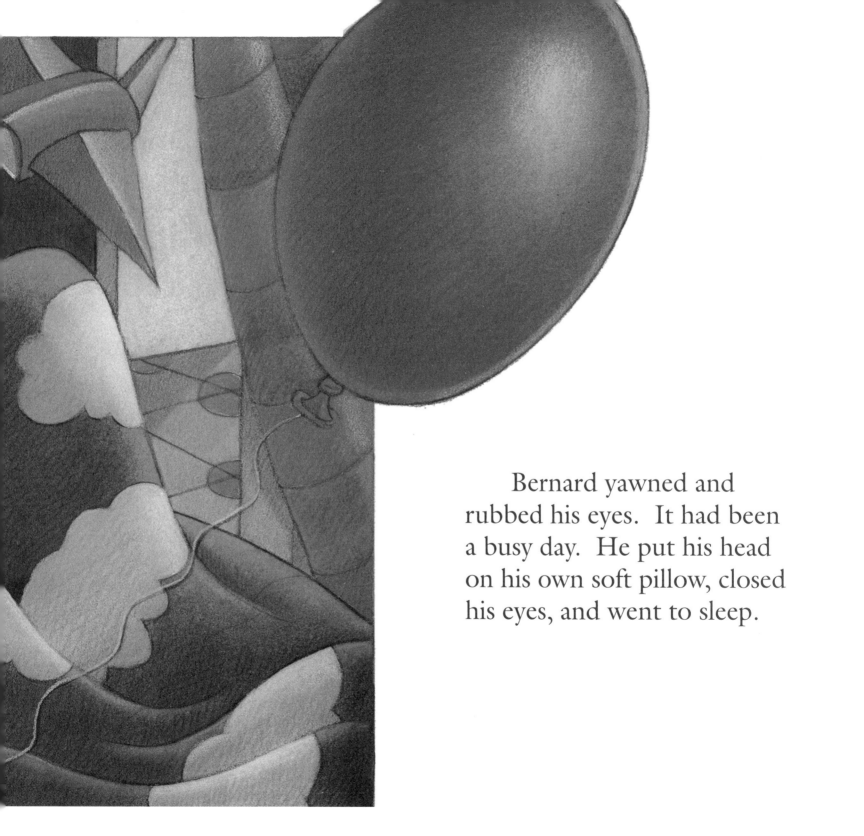

Bernard yawned and rubbed his eyes. It had been a busy day. He put his head on his own soft pillow, closed his eyes, and went to sleep.